Walt Disney Pictures'

OLIVER & Company

The More the Merrier

By Justine Korman
Illustrated by Willy Ito and Ron Dias

A GOLDEN BOOK • NEW YORK
Western Publishing Company, Inc., Racine, Wisconsin 53404

Library of Congress Catalog Card Number: 88-80739 ISBN: 0-307-11731-6/ISBN: 0-307-61731-9 (lib. bdg.)
A B C D E F G H I J K L M

Winston, the butler, gently opened Georgette's door.

"Rise and shine, Georgette," he said, pulling open the drapes on her satin dog bed.

Georgette, a pampered poodle, yawned and stretched. She had slept late again.

Georgette hated the lonely mornings when her eight-year-old owner, Jenny, was at school. She got up and looked in her mirror.

"My eyes are all puffy from sleeping too long," Georgette said with a sigh. Then she fussed with her powder, curlers, and brush until the image staring back at her from the heart-shaped mirror was poodle perfect.

Georgette's ears perked up when she heard sounds from downstairs.

"It's Jenny!" Georgette cried. Her heart leapt, her legs went all frisky, and her pom-pom tail wagged wildly.

"Dignity, dignity," Georgette reminded herself as she sauntered downstairs to greet Jenny.

Georgette found Jenny in the kitchen, crouched on the floor.

"You must be hungry," Jenny coaxed, pushing a plate toward a shy little kitten under the chair.

"That's my dish!" Georgette realized with horror.

Then Winston called Jenny to the phone, leaving Georgette alone with the kitten.

"Ahem," Georgette said. "Do you know whose dish that is?"

"Uh...yours?" the kitten mumbled through a mouthful of food.

"And do you know whose home this is?" Georgette hissed.

"J-J-Jenny's," the cat stammered.

Georgette glared at the kitten. "Everything from the doorknobs down is *mine*!"

Jenny returned, grinning.

"Guess what, Oliver? My parents said you can stay!"
Jenny told the kitten. Oliver glanced nervously from Jenny
to Georgette.

"I see you two have met," Jenny continued. "I know
you're going to be good friends."

As soon as they were alone again Georgette told the kitten, "I don't care what Jenny says. This is my house, not yours. So why don't you just go back where you came from?"

"I'd rather stay here with Jenny," Oliver explained. "She loves me more than Fagin's gang does."

"Fagin's gang?" Georgette asked disgustedly.

So Oliver described how he had made friends with a street-smart dog named Dodger and the rest of Fagin's gang of cunning canines.

"They sound like a...colorful group," Georgette sneered.

"They were nicer to me than you are," Oliver replied. "And they were willing to share what little they had."

Later that day, when it was time for Jenny to practice the piano, Oliver skipped across the keys and made the little girl laugh.

"You and me together," Jenny and Oliver sang.

Georgette sulked in the corner and thought, "Jenny doesn't love me anymore."

When her practicing was over, Jenny suggested, "Let's all go to the park!"

But Georgette refused to be seen with a cat. So Jenny and Oliver went out alone.

Georgette felt even worse when the two returned, all giggles and purrs.

"You missed a great time, Georgette," Jenny said. "And look at Oliver's pretty new collar and I.D. tag!"

Georgette winced when Oliver showed her the tag that said, "My name is Oliver" and gave Jenny's address as his home.

"Not for long," Georgette thought. "Somehow I'll get rid of that cat!"

The next morning Georgette looked in her mirror and screamed. Her reflection wasn't the only one she saw. Several tough-looking dogs stood behind her.

"How did you get in here?" she demanded.

"Relax! We just came to get our cat," Dodger explained.

"You must be Fagin's gang," Georgette said. "I'll be more than happy to help you get Oliver back."

"Something's going on around here," Winston grumbled. He started upstairs to investigate the doggy sounds he was hearing.

"Quick, hide!" Georgette commanded.

The gang vanished just seconds before Winston opened
the door and peeked into Georgette's room. She pretended
to be sleeping, but under the blanket were various members
of Fagin's gang. Somehow Winston didn't notice the extra
paws sticking out of Georgette's blanket, or even the new
dog "statue" holding up a potted plant.

As soon as Winston was gone Georgette flung back the blanket and said, "Hurry! I'll show you where to find your cat."

The dogs tiptoed to Jenny's room, where Oliver was curled up asleep on the bed.

"He looks awfully happy," said Rita, the almost-Afghan hound. "Maybe we should forget the whole thing."

"You can't!" Georgette said with a gasp. "I mean, he's miserable here!"

Then, without anyone seeing, Georgette pinched Oliver. The cat sprang up out of a sound sleep and squealed, "Ouch!"

Then before he could say anything else, Oliver was stuffed into a pillowcase. The gang carried him down the fire escape and back to Fagin's headquarters near the docks.

Georgette rubbed her manicured paws together and said, "Alone at last!"

When Jenny came home, she looked all over for Oliver. She called and called and searched under every bed and in every closet.

"He must have run away, Miss," Winston told Jenny. But Jenny just couldn't believe that. "Oliver loves me, and he knows I love him. He wouldn't just leave. Would he, Georgette?"

Then Jenny hugged Georgette and cried into her soft, curly fur.

"At least I still have you," Jenny sobbed.

Georgette suddenly realized that she'd done something stupid. "If I don't help her get that cat back," she thought to herself, "she's going to get me soaking wet."

Before Georgette could think of a way to find Oliver, a note came from Fagin. It said that the kitten had been found and would be returned, in exchange for a big reward. Fagin's note told Jenny to bring the reward money to the docks.

Jenny and Georgette set off through the rough streets of Fagin's neighborhood. Finally they reached the docks.

When Jenny met Fagin, she said, "Here is your reward. It's all I have." Jenny held out her piggy bank.

Fagin felt ashamed of himself and gave Oliver back to Jenny. "I don't want the reward," he said.

Jenny and the kitten hugged each other.

Jenny was happy again. "Georgette helped me find you," she said to Oliver. "Aren't you going to kiss her, too?"

Georgette winked at Oliver. And when he rubbed his head against hers, she whispered, "I guess we're stuck with each other, cat. Everything from the doorknobs down is yours, too."

Georgette was soon surprised to discover she liked having a cat around the house. To Winston's dismay, they chased each other all over the place.

"Exercise is so good for the complexion," Georgette panted.

And when Jenny practiced the piano, Georgette and Oliver sang their own duet while Winston covered his ears.

Favorite GOLDEN Look-Look® Books:

Written and illustrated by Mercer Mayer:

Written and illustrated by Richard Scarry:

ISBN: 0-307-1